CONSTRUCTION

SALLY SUTTON · ILLUSTRATED BY BRIAN LOVELOCK

WALKER BOOKS

Dig the ground. Dig the ground.

Bore down in the mud.

Shove the piles in one by one.

Fill the holes. Fill the holes.

Let the concrete drop.

Spread it fast before it sets.

Hoist the wood. Hoist the wood.

Chain and hook and strap.

Swing it round, then lower it down.

Thonk!
CLONK!
CLAP!

Cut the planks. Cut the planks.

Measure, mark and saw.

Earmuffs will protect your ears.

Wizz!

Zizz!

ROAR!

Build the frame. Build the frame.

Hammer all day long.

Make the stairs and floors and walls.

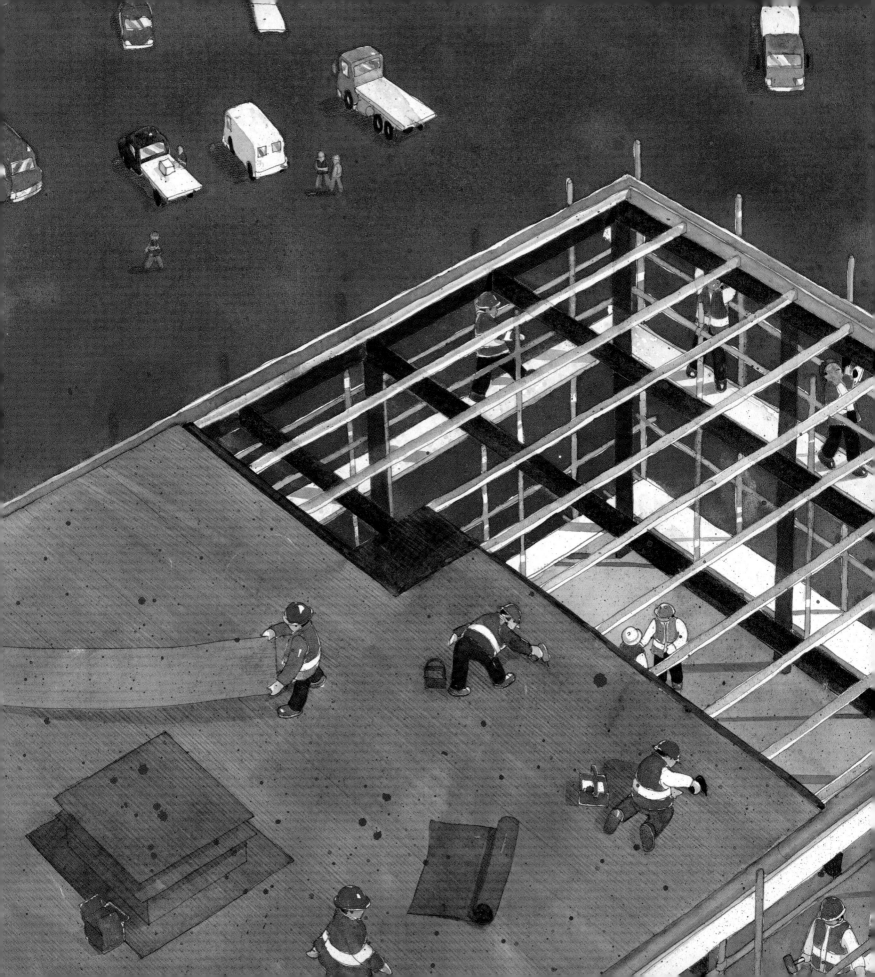

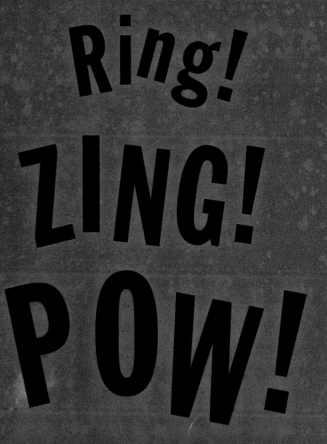

Raise the roof. Raise the roof.

Drive the screws in now.

Power tools will do the job.

Ring!
ZING!
POW!

Build the sides. Build the sides.

Fit the doors in too.

Lift the windows

into place.

Lay the pipes. Lay the pipes.

Twist and turn and click.

Run the wires so you'll have power.

Scritch!

SWITCH!

FLICK!

Spread the paint. Spread the paint.

Bend and stretch and stoop.

Dry one coat, then start the next.

Glug!
GLOP!
GLOOP!

Fill the rooms. Fill the rooms.

Join the hustle-bustle.

Chairs and tables, shelves and books.

Choose your books. Choose your books.

Borrow all you need.

The library's here for everyone.

FACTS

LOADER CRANE: A loader crane has an articulated arm that is used to load and unload heavy things.

MOBILE CRANE: A truck-mounted crane that can lift heavy materials from one place to another. It can move up and down and swing from side to side.

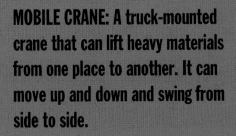

EXCAVATOR: Excavators dig the ground. This excavator has an auger attachment. It drills holes for the building's foundation piles.

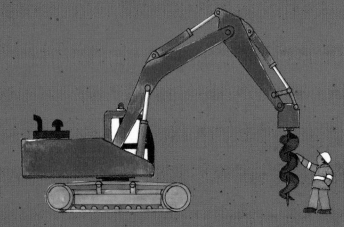

CONSTRUCTION WORKER

Hard hat

Safety glasses

Earmuffs →

← High-visibility vest

Safety gloves →

← Steelcapped safety boots

Builders on a big construction site need lots of special clothing and equipment to stay safe.

CONCRETE PUMPING TRUCK: A pumping truck has a long boom. The boom moves around to pump wet concrete through a hose to any part of the construction site.

CONCRETE MIXING TRUCK: This truck mixes cement, sand and gravel to make liquid concrete. It feeds the concrete into a pumping truck.